X 363.232 GRE

Green, Sara, 1964-
Bomb-sniffing dogs

BER

4/2015

ST. MARY PARISH LIBRARY
FRANKLIN, LOUISIANA

DOGS TO THE RESCUE!
BOMB-SNIFFING DOGS

By Sara Green

BELLWETHER MEDIA • MINNEAPOLIS, MN

Jump into the cockpit and take flight with **Pilot books**. Your journey will take you on high-energy adventures as you learn about all that is wild, weird, fascinating, and fun!

This edition first published in 2014 by Bellwether Media, Inc.

No part of this publication may be reproduced in whole or in part without written permission of the publisher. For information regarding permission, write to Bellwether Media, Inc., Attention: Permissions Department, 5357 Penn Avenue South, Minneapolis, MN 55419.

Library of Congress Cataloging-in-Publication Data

Green, Sara, 1964-
 Bomb-sniffing dogs / by Sara Green.
    pages cm. – (Pilot: Dogs to the rescue!)
 Includes bibliographical references and index.
 Summary: "Engaging images accompany information about bomb-sniffing dogs. The combination of high-interest subject matter and narrative text is intended for students in grades 3 through 7"–Provided by publisher.
 ISBN 978-1-60014-954-2 (hardcover : alk. paper)
1. Police dogs–Juvenile literature. 2. Search dogs–Juvenile literature. 3. Detector dogs–Juvenile literature. I. Title.
 HV8025.G734 2014
 363.2'32–dc23
                                                                    2013002288

Text copyright © 2014 by Bellwether Media, Inc. PILOT and associated logos are trademarks and/or registered trademarks of Bellwether Media, Inc. SCHOLASTIC, CHILDREN'S PRESS, and associated logos are trademarks and/or registered trademarks of Scholastic Inc.

Printed in the United States of America, North Mankato, MN.

TABLE OF CONTENTS

A Hero Saves the Day 4
A Nose That Knows 6
On the Job 10
Trained to Sniff 12
A Team Effort 16
Layka: A Special Forces Hero 20
Glossary 22
To Learn More 23
Index 24

A HERO SAVES THE DAY

Passengers hurry to catch their flights at a busy New York City airport. They do not realize that their lives are in danger. Someone has made a bomb threat over the telephone. The caller threatened to **detonate** bombs that would blow up several airplanes.

Police quickly bring Brandy, a specially trained German Shepherd, onto an airplane. The dog uses her sensitive nose to sniff for **explosives**. She sniffs a black briefcase in the cockpit and sits down next to it. This is the signal! Brandy has smelled a bomb. A team of **bomb technicians** rushes to the plane. They find enough explosives inside the briefcase to destroy the plane. They **disarm** the bomb minutes before it is set to explode. The brave German Shepherd saved many lives that day!

A NOSE THAT KNOWS

People began to train dogs to be bomb sniffers in the 1970s. Dogs have an excellent sense of smell and can cover a large area in a short amount of time. Trained dogs can smell and find explosives much faster than people. Bomb-sniffing dogs learn to identify different explosives, weapons, and materials used to make bombs. These include dynamite, gunpowder, and plastic explosives.

Three dog breeds are commonly used as bomb-sniffing dogs. They are German Shepherds, Labrador Retrievers, and Belgian Malinois. Springer Spaniels and Vizslas also make great bomb-sniffing dogs. All of these breeds are known for their energy, intelligence, and loyalty. Bomb-sniffing dogs must have other qualities, too. They must be able to stay calm in crowds. They also need to enjoy playing because finding explosives is like a game.

Get a Whiff

Dogs have up to 60 times more receptor cells in their noses than people. Their sense of smell is thousands of times more sensitive than a human's!

Breeds of Bomb-Sniffing Dogs

German Shepherd

Labrador Retriever

Belgian Malinois

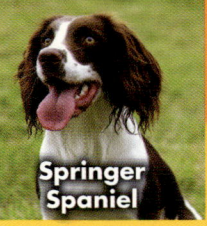
Springer Spaniel

Vizsla

Bomb-sniffing dogs work in a variety of places. Many patrol busy airports, bus stations, and subways. They are often present at sports stadiums or other places that draw large crowds. Bomb-sniffing dogs search for explosives at events attended by important people, such as the President of the United States. They check schools and other buildings when there is a bomb scare.

Keeping People Safe

Every day in the United States, hundreds of bomb-sniffing dog teams patrol major transportation systems. This includes the nation's 39 busiest airports.

Profile: German Shepherd

Size
Height: 22 to 26 inches
(56 to 66 centimeters)

Weight: 50 to 95 pounds
(23 to 43 kilograms)

Intelligence
The German Shepherd is the third smartest dog breed. The dog will obey new commands almost immediately.

Sensitive Nose
The dog can detect a teaspoon of sugar in a million gallons of water. This is equal to two Olympic-sized swimming pools.

The United States **Border Patrol** also uses bomb-sniffing dogs. The dogs help prevent weapons and explosives from entering the U.S. from other countries. They sniff passengers and luggage arriving on ships. They also nose around cars at border crossings and cargo in warehouses. If someone is trying to **smuggle** explosives into the U.S., a bomb-sniffing dog will know.

ON THE JOB

One of the most common places to find explosives is in war zones. Homemade bombs called improvised explosive devices, or IEDs, are among the most dangerous. The enemy hides IEDs in buildings, roads, and fields. The bombs explode when people step on them or vehicles drive over them. However, bomb-sniffing dogs can detect IEDs. For this reason, many countries use bomb-sniffing dogs in their militaries. The dogs' sharp sense of smell helps keep troops safe.

Military bomb-sniffing dogs face many risks. They are in danger of explosives-related injuries and being shot by the enemy. Extreme weather conditions can also hit the dogs hard. Many bomb-sniffing dogs work in the desert. Summer temperatures there can soar to more than 120 degrees Fahrenheit (49 degrees Celsius). The troops must protect the dogs against **dehydration** and **heat stroke**. The dogs often wear goggles to protect their eyes from sand.

TRAINED TO SNIFF

Bomb-sniffing dogs go to special training schools. Most enter when they are between one and three years old. The dogs learn to recognize the different explosives their noses will smell on the job. Training lasts for up to six months. It covers bomb-sniffing skills and how to work with a **handler**. The handlers always use **positive reinforcement** when they train their dogs. They give the dogs a lot of praise for their efforts!

Keeping People Safe

Lackland Air Force Base in Texas is known for training dogs for military work. Every year, Lackland trains about 300 detection dogs to sniff for drugs or bombs.

At first, handlers place items that smell like explosives in front of the dogs. The dogs learn to sit after they smell the explosives. This is called a **passive response**. Over time, the dogs learn the scents of a variety of explosives. Then handlers hide real explosives in places such as luggage and cabinets. The dogs must find the explosives on their own. When they can do this, the dogs will become **certified**. Now they are ready to work in the real world!

Bomb-sniffing dogs stick to business when they are working. They do not let food, people, loud noises, or other dogs distract them. The dogs search for explosives without barking or whining. They sit quietly to alert their handlers that an explosive is nearby. Every year, bomb-sniffing dogs must pass a special test to be recertified.

The dogs always receive a reward for finding an explosive. Each agency that uses bomb-sniffing dogs decides how to best reward its dogs. Some dogs receive food. Others are rewarded with a toy and playtime. Bomb-sniffing dogs do not demand much in return for saving so many lives!

A TEAM EFFORT

These specially trained dogs live with their handlers. Handlers are not regular dog trainers. They have special skills and knowledge about explosives. Most handlers have a background in the military, law enforcement, or security. Handlers must be able to communicate well with their dogs. They need excellent people skills to deal with stressful situations in public. Handlers also have responsibilities at home. They must practice with their dogs every week to keep the dogs' skills sharp. Knowledge of first aid is also important for treating any dog injuries.

Foreign Speak
Some handlers teach their dogs commands in a foreign language. The foreign language acts like a secret code.

Bomb-sniffing dogs usually **retire** when they are between 8 and 10 years old. Many dogs continue to live with their handlers. Sometimes loving families adopt the dogs.

Many bomb-sniffing dogs face new challenges after they retire. The habit of sniffing for explosives may remain strong. Some retired dogs feel the urge to search for bombs in dog parks and their own yards.

Post-traumatic stress disorder, or PTSD, affects many retired bomb-sniffing dogs. This condition causes dogs to frighten easily. Many become aggressive or shy. Loud noises may remind them of battlefield explosions and gunfire. The dogs may refuse to enter certain buildings. **Veterinarians** can help dogs recover from PTSD. With time and care, most dogs can live normal lives. They enjoy their peaceful retirements far away from danger.

LAYKA: A SPECIAL FORCES HERO

Layka is a bomb-sniffing Belgian Malinois. She is also a military hero. In 2012, Layka was on patrol with a U.S. Special Forces unit in Afghanistan. The soldiers came to a **suspicious** building. Layka entered first to sniff for explosives and look for the enemy. As soon as she went inside, Layka was **ambushed**! An enemy soldier shot Layka in her leg and her stomach, but the dog fought back. She held on to the attacker until U.S. soldiers could capture him.

Layka was quickly flown to a veterinary hospital in the United States. She lost her leg but earned a medal for her bravery. Layka retired from the military and began a new life at home with her handler. Thanks to Layka, the lives of many soldiers were saved. They will never forget this heroic canine bomb sniffer.

GLOSSARY

ambushed—attacked suddenly by people who were hiding

bomb technicians—people who disarm or dispose of bombs and other explosives

Border Patrol—a group of people who check what enters and exits a country

certified—recognized as having mastered specific job skills

dehydration—excessive loss of water from the body

detonate—to make something explode

disarm—to make an explosive harmless

explosives—materials that can explode and cause damage and injury

handler—a person who is responsible for a highly trained dog

heat stroke—a life-threatening condition caused by too much exposure to sun and hot temperatures

passive response—a calm, quiet response

positive reinforcement—using treats, toys, or other rewards to praise good behavior

retire—to stop working

smuggle—to bring into a country illegally

suspicious—something that appears to be wrong

veterinarians—doctors who treat animals

TO LEARN MORE

AT THE LIBRARY
Barnes, Julia. *Dogs at Work*. Milwaukee, Wis.: Gareth Stevens Pub., 2006.

Goldish, Meish. *Bomb-Sniffing Dogs*. New York, N.Y.: Bearport Pub., 2012.

Meyer, Karl. *Dog Heroes: A Story Poster Book*. North Adams, Mass.: Storey Publishing, 2008.

ON THE WEB
Learning more about bomb-sniffing dogs is as easy as 1, 2, 3.

1. Go to www.factsurfer.com.

2. Enter "bomb-sniffing dogs" into the search box.

3. Click the "Surf" button and you will see a list of related Web sites.

With factsurfer.com, finding more information is just a click away.

INDEX

adoption, 18
Afghanistan, 20
airports, 4, 8
Belgian Malinois, 6, 7, 20
Brandy, 4
breeds, 4, 6, 7, 9, 20
certification, 13, 15
characteristics, 6, 9
distractions, 15
drugs, 13
equipment, 10
German Shepherd, 4, 6, 7, 9
handlers, 12, 13, 15, 16, 17, 18, 20
history, 4, 6, 20
IEDs, 10
Lackland Air Force Base, 13
languages, 17
Layka, 20
military dogs, 10, 13, 20
passive response, 4, 13, 15
post-traumatic stress disorder, 19
retirement, 18, 19, 20
rewards, 12, 15
risks, 10, 19, 20
safety, 10, 16, 20
sense of smell, 4, 6, 7, 9, 10, 12
training, 12, 13
United States Border Patrol, 9
veterinarians, 19, 20
weapons, 6, 9

The images in this book are reproduced through the courtesy of: Eric Isselee, front cover (left), p. 9; Teh Eng Koon/ AFP/ Getty Images/ Newscom, front cover; Monika Wisniewska, p. 4; AFP/ Getty Images, pp. 5, 8, 11, 12; Bill Pugliano/ Stringer/ Getty Images, p. 7; Peter Kunasz, p. 7 (top); Capture Light, p. 7 (middle top); Rolf Klebsattel, p. 7 (middle); Paul D Smith, p. 7 (middle bottom); AnetaPics, p. 7 (bottom); US Air Force/ Derek Kaufman, p. 10; Ralph Lauer/ KRT/ Newscom, p. 13; Itar-Tass Photo Agency/ Alamy, p. 14; Mark Avery/ ZUMA Press/ Newscom, p. 15; Getty Images, p. 16; Daniel Wallace/ ZUMA Press/ Newscom, p. 17; AP Photo/ Gregory Bull, p. 18; Charlie Neuman/ ZUMA Press/ Newscom, p. 19; US Department of Defense, p. 21.